WHERE'S DUDLEY?

Anne Schraff

SADDLEBACK PAGETURNERS • MYSTERY •

PAGETURNERS

ADVENTURE

A Horse Called Courage

Planet Doom

The Terrible Orchid Sky

Up Rattler Mountain

Who Has Seen the Beast?

MYSTERY

The Hunter

Once Upon a Crime

Whatever Happened
to Megan Marie?

When Sleeping Dogs Awaken

Where's Dudley?

Development and Production: Laurel Associates, Inc.
Cover Illustrator: Black Eagle Productions

SADDLEBACK
PUBLISHING • INC.
Three Watson
Irvine, CA 92618-2767

Website: www.sdlback.com

ISBN 1-56254-177-3

Printed in the United States of America
09 08 07 06 05   9 8 7 6 5 4 3 2

CONTENTS

Chapter 1 5

Chapter 2 12

Chapter 3 17

Chapter 4 24

Chapter 5 34

Chapter 6 40

Chapter 7 50

Chapter 8 60

Chapter 9 64

Chapter 10 69

Chapter 1

Tony Young had spent all morning in college classes and the rest of the day delivering pizzas. He had just gotten home and was getting ready for a nice hot shower when the phone rang.

"Yeah?" Tony answered in a slightly annoyed way.

"Tony, don't say anything about what happened in history class today," Brandi Ketchum said in a frightened voice. "Don't say a *word*—especially to the police if they come around!"

"Huh?" Tony gulped. "What're you talking about, Brandi?"

"Gotta go! Just don't tell anyone *anything* about what happened in Dudley's class today," Brandi said before she hung up.

Tony didn't get it. He wondered if the phone call was some kind of a joke. As he showered, he thought about Mr. Walter Dudley's world history class that morning. For Tony, it was always the longest class of the day for a very simple reason. Dudley was boring and dictatorial. Even the slightest little overheard whisper was cause for a stern lecture. The old guy acted as if he were teaching grade schoolers instead of adults. He didn't give his students a bit of respect.

"Today's kids are so lucky," Dudley would say bitterly. "At your age I was fighting for my country! Although Mr. Dudley gave tough tests, he didn't often lecture about the material in the book. He rambled on about one thing and another, always with a negative slant on things. Sometimes he told war stories. The kids guessed that his sour temper was the result of the wounded leg that still caused him to limp.

But what could have happened this

morning that upset Brandi so much? For one thing, their tests had been passed back. Tony was grateful for his C plus, but he had heard a lot of groaning around him. Just before Tony left, several students were crowding Dudley's desk, arguing about their bad grades. Maybe the argument had turned bitter, but Tony hadn't heard anything unusual.

Tony shrugged and watched some TV. Then he got dressed in a polo shirt and new jeans for his date with Dawna Reston. Dawna was 20, just two years younger than Tony. Tonight they were planning to take in a movie and then stop for tacos.

When Tony had started his junior year last September, Dawna was a freshman, but she had dropped out since then. Now she worked at a quickie haircut shop and talked a lot about getting married soon.

Tony didn't want to get married anytime soon. He *liked* Dawna. She was a beautiful girl, and he was proud of her when they went places. They surfed together a lot, and enjoyed the same kinds of music—jazz, rock, country.

Tony had been surfing since he was 12, but Dawna had learned the sport just since they'd been dating. Now she loved to hit the waves as much as Tony did.

Over tacos, Dawna said, "Wasn't that movie romantic? Wasn't it sweet how that guy followed his girlfriend all the way to Australia to win her heart?"

"I don't know. He seemed sorta stupid to me," Tony said.

"Tony! Didn't it touch your heart that a guy would go to such desperate lengths to win the girl of his dreams?" Dawna cried.

"He leaves his good job, he gets kicked by a kangaroo, he falls in the ocean . . . he was a jerk," Tony laughed. Then, seeing that Dawna looked hurt, he quickly tried to change the subject. "Want to go out to the beach and catch the waves on Saturday?" he asked.

"Maybe," Dawna said, a pouty look clouding her face. She fell into bad moods easily. If she hadn't been so gorgeous, Tony would have dumped her long ago. He liked happier people who didn't get their feelings hurt so easily.

At world history class on Wednesday, Mr. Dudley didn't show up at all. Remembering Brandi's frantic call, Tony glanced back at her. The poor girl looked *stricken*. She gave Tony a desperate look that seemed to say, "Remember what I said—not a word about what happened in class!"

"I wonder where Dudley is," Tony said to Chaz Spender, the guy who sat next to him.

Chaz made a wry face. "Weren't you here on Monday?" he asked.

"Well, sure . . . but what was so special about Monday?" Tony asked.

"See you after class," Chaz said.

The substitute teacher showed a

movie on World War II. Then, after class, Tony and Chaz walked down to the fruit machines.

"Didn't you hear about it, Tony? A bunch of students flunked that test," Chaz explained. "Three of them got in a big fight with Dudley. Man, it was ugly. MacCarr, he's going, 'You senile old man, maybe you're not fit to teach anymore!' Then Brandi and her friend Lisa *really* let him have it. They told Dudley to do everybody a favor and drop dead."

"Man, I guess I was gone by then," Tony said, picking a red apple from the machine. "What did Dudley say?"

"He was fuming! He said he didn't have to take that kind of disrespectful talk. The last I saw him he was sort of speed-limping down the walk toward the faculty parking lot. I think he was gonna get security. The three of them—Mac and the girls—were following after him. I had to go to work then, so I don't know what happened out in the parking lot. But when I saw Brandi later on, she looked really scared. You know, like she'd seen a ghost or something. . . ."

Chapter 2

"So what do you think? Where's Dudley now?" Tony asked.

"The man just disappeared. His car hasn't been moved from his parking space since Monday," Chaz said. "Come on, I'll show you."

There was a yellow ribbon around Dudley's car, and several police cars were parked around it. It was a crime scene!

"Oh, man," Tony groaned, "don't tell me those idiot kids were so mad at Dudley that they . . . did something to harm him."

"I looked in the car before the cops arrived," Chaz said. "There was no body in there, but I saw some stuff on the front seat. I couldn't be sure . . . but it looked like it might have been blood."

"*Blood?*" Tony gasped.

"Yeah," Chaz said. "I haven't talked to anybody who saw what happened, but I bet there was a really big fight. When I saw those kids, they were walking right behind him, yelling their heads off. Maybe the old guy gave off a choice insult, and you know—maybe they *did* something to him."

"Come on, Chaz, you're getting carried away!" Tony laughed. "It doesn't make sense that kids would bash in a teacher's head just because of some stupid test grade!"

Chaz shrugged. "I don't know, Tony. Maybe ol' Dudley just went too far. *All* of us were pretty fed up with him, of course. He would never talk about the subject matter, and then he'd give us these monster tests, and lots of kids would flunk!" Chaz said.

After his last class, Tony headed for his VW in the student parking lot.

Brandi rushed up to him, grabbing his arm. "Tony! You heard about Dudley, huh?" she asked breathlessly.

"Yeah, I heard that Mr. Dudley is missing," Tony said.

"We said some awful things to him Monday—but we didn't *do* anything to him! All we did was yell at him and he stomped off to his car and climbed in and . . . who knows? Maybe he bumped his head on the doorframe, because I saw blood on his head. But *we* didn't do anything!"

"Brandi, I don't know anything about this. I don't want to get mixed up in it, okay?" Tony said.

"But Tony, you've got to help me. The cops are talking to everybody, and if you heard anything, just don't tell them the awful things we said. We didn't mean that we really wanted him dead!" Brandi cried.

"Brandi, I *didn't* hear or see anything Monday, okay?" Tony assured her. "But one guy in our class has already told me that he saw you and Mac and Lisa following Dudley to his car. . . ."

"Who saw that?" Brandi gasped, her eyes growing huge with fear.

"Just some guy. I don't remember his name," Tony lied. "Look, Brandi—people have arguments every day. If something bad happened to Dudley, it probably had nothing to do with his students."

Mac and Lisa joined them then. They both looked as nervous as Brandi did.

"Hey, Tony," Mac said, "I've been looking for you. If the cops ask you any questions, just tell them *all* the kids hated Dudley, not just us."

"Yeah," Lisa joined in. "If Dudley is dead, I think every one of us would give each other high fives."

"Why don't you *shut up*, you airhead!" Mac snapped.

"Just because we yelled at him doesn't mean we killed him," Lisa said defensively.

Tony grabbed the door handle of his VW. "This has nothing to do with me, you guys. I got to go deliver pizzas." Then he jumped in his car and peeled out. The whole thing was giving him a headache. As he drove away, he looked back at Brandi, Lisa, and Mac.

Tony didn't know the three well, but he'd seen them around the campus during the past three years. He didn't particularly *like* any of them—but he never thought they were the kind of people who could do somebody in. But then he didn't *really* know them, either. And Mr. Dudley's body wasn't in the car . . . so maybe a crime hadn't been committed at all.

Except that Dudley had apparently vanished into thin air. And why was there blood on the seat of his car?

Chapter 3

On Friday, the students in Mr. Dudley's world history class were questioned by the police. Tony was glad he didn't know anything about what had gone down. The detective let him go in about five minutes.

On Saturday, Tony picked up Dawna early, and they headed for the beach with their boards. When they reached the sand, Tony grinned. "Hey, looks good, huh? Lots of rolling waves. They're better to catch than the pitching ones," he said.

"Hey, you know what, Tony?" Dawna said. "My sister goes to your college. She said there's a big rumor going around. There's supposed to be a little group of students who plotted to kill Mr. Dudley, that history teacher who's missing. My sister told me they haven't found his body yet—but they're pretty sure he's dead. You have Dudley for a class, don't you?"

"Yeah, but that stuff your sister is hearing—that's just wild talk. Nobody knows anything for sure about what happened to the guy. It's a fact that Dudley had a fight with some students over a test. But that doesn't mean they were plotting to *kill* him. That gossip is just nonsense," Tony said.

"But my sister said they found buckets of blood in the teacher's car, so he *must* be dead," Dawna chattered on excitedly.

"Ah, Dawna, every time somebody else repeats a wild story, it gets gorier and crazier. I know a guy who saw the blood, and he said there were just a few smudges," Tony said.

Dawna paused, clutching her surfboard under her arm. "Well, my sister is *sure* he's dead. She said this little group of kids just couldn't wait to get rid of that poor old teacher because he was so demanding," she insisted.

"Ha! Probably old Dudley is in Ensenada right now, balancing a margarita on his stomach and enjoying the view," Tony laughed.

"Tony," Dawna said critically, "don't you take anything seriously? Sometimes I think you're a very shallow person. You need to work on that, Tony. I'm talking about a murder, and you're giggling about margaritas!"

"Come on, baby, let's hit the waves. You got your sunblock on?" Tony asked.

Dawna frowned. "Yes, I have my sunblock on," she said in a miffed voice, "but I think you ought to be a little bit serious, Tony—especially when it comes to a tragedy like this!"

The sun was shining, and the water was about 65 degrees. The waves were perfect. Since Dawna was still a beginner, Tony was glad the waves were running only about three feet. He hoped she wouldn't spoil their whole day by whining on and on about Walter Dudley.

Dawna walked into the surf and soon picked her wave. When she was just the right distance out, she turned back toward the shore, lying on her board, paddling. When the wave came, Dawna grabbed the rails of the surfboard and pushed herself into a squatting position. Tony grinned. She was a fast learner, and Tony had been a good teacher. In a few seconds, Dawna was up and flying on her board. She was doing beautifully, even dismounting the board like an expert before hitting the sand.

"Way to go, girl!" Tony shouted, heading into the water himself. The waves were getting a little friskier. For a half hour or so, Tony rode to shore on five-footers. He relished the luxury of having the water to themselves, but it didn't last long. Soon other surfers began appearing.

Dawna spread a big towel on the sand and sat down. "Was I really okay, Tony? You're not just saying that, are you?" She said flirtatiously.

"You were great, Dawna," Tony said, sitting beside her.

Dawna was silent a moment, but then she said, "Tony, tell me something. Did you *like* Mr. Dudley?"

Tony groaned inwardly. Not Dudley again! Even vanished, the guy was a pest! "No, Dawna. Nobody did. He was about as interesting as a guy reading the daily stock market results in a monotone. To tell you the truth, he was the worst teacher I ever had," Tony said.

"Why do you talk about him in the past tense, Tony?" Dawna asked.

"I don't know. I didn't even think about it," Tony answered.

Dawna's eyes narrowed. "I bet some of your friends already told you what happened, huh, Tony?" she said in a suspicious, accusing tone.

"What? Are you saying I *know* all about a murder, and I'm keeping quiet about it for some reason?" Tony demanded.

"Well, no—but you *must* have heard stuff. My sister said everybody is talking about it. A lot of kids must know," Dawna said.

"Your sister is a regular little rumor machine, isn't she?" Tony said. "I'm too busy trying to pass my classes to get into that silly kind of stuff."

Again, Dawna looked hurt. "Tina doesn't lie. She said that at lunch, a senior guy told her that some kids had been plotting to kill Mr. Dudley for weeks. The guy said he heard this group discussing where they'd hide the body once they killed him. One of the plotters was thinking they should dump him in the mountains and—"

"Dawna, knock it off!" Tony barked.

"This is absolutely *nuts*! If your sister's friend heard stuff like that, it was just somebody's sick humor."

"Well, I think it's awful for people to even joke about such stuff," Dawna said indignantly. "I certainly hope *you* don't sit around with your friends, joking about things like that."

Tony leaned back and patted the damp sand. "Hey, the sand is just the right consistency for a sand castle. Why don't you build one for me, babe?"

"You're making fun of me, aren't you?" Dawna said in a pouty voice.

"Nah. I just don't want Dudley's ghost to spoil a perfectly good day." He knew he shouldn't have said that the minute the words were out of his mouth. He felt like slapping himself.

"Mr. Dudley's ghost?" Dawna gasped. "See? You *know* he's dead!"

Chapter 4

Just then, Tony saw Mac and Lisa walking down the beach. They were surfers, too. In fact, Tony and his old girlfriend, Marcy, had often seen Mac and Lisa surfing from this spot.

"Hi, Tony!" Lisa called out.

"How're the waves today, man?" Mac asked.

"Great!" Tony called back.

Before they could overhear, Dawna whispered to Tony, "Are they part of that group that fought with Mr. Dudley?"

"No, no," Tony said hurriedly.

Neither Lisa nor Mac knew Dawna, so Tony introduced them. For some reason, Dawna seemed a little cool. When Mac and Lisa walked into the white soup with their boards, she leaned toward Tony and said, "My sister said that one of the cops' suspects is a guy named *Mac*. I wonder if that guy's the one. I don't like him. Something about him just gives me the creeps."

Tony had had just about enough of Dawna's obsession with Dudley. "Aw, Dawna, give it a rest," he pleaded.

"I bet it *is* the guy," Dawna said grimly. "I have a gut feeling that it's him. I hope he's not a good friend of yours."

"Dawna, I see Mac and Lisa in class, and once or twice I've seen them here on the beach—but they're not my friends," Tony said.

It turned out that Lisa and Mac were lousy surfers. After paddling out to the peaking waves, they got into a conflict with some other surfers. One hairy surfer almost ran Lisa down, and then got into a shouting match with Mac. Tony was surprised to see that Mac and Lisa were crowding the other surfers.

25

They'd been around often enough to know the rules of the water.

"Oh, man, Mac and Lisa are acting like newcomers," Tony said. "They should be riding in the soup instead of demanding the right of way."

"It's no wonder they can't behave in a civilized way in the water," Dawna said in a judgmental, snippy way. She had already made up her mind about Mac and Lisa. Because she didn't like them, she was sure they had found a way to get rid of their history teacher. And now they were bullying some innocent surfers.

When Mac and Lisa finally came ashore for a break, some big, tattooed surfers gave them the stinkeye. To Tony's displeasure, Mac and Lisa joined him and Dawna. His girlfriend looked at them as if they were twin stingrays.

"There are sure a lotta creeps surfing today," Mac said. "Did you see the way they acted out there? What bozos!"

"Well, there are rules for surfers, you know," Dawna said icily. "You two have to show respect to other people, too."

Surprised at the girl's tone, Lisa stared coldy at her. "I've never seen you at school, Dawna. Are you a freshman this year?"

"I don't *go* to school," Dawna said in a frosty voice. "I have a job." Then, frowning and glancing over at Tony, she said, "Can we go now?"

Mac looked confused. What had caused the hostility between the two girls? "Are we *bothering* you guys?" he asked. "We can go sit somewhere else. . . ."

Tony was embarrassed by Dawna's rudeness. "No, no, it's fine," he said hurriedly. The truth was that he wasn't crazy about Mac and Lisa joining them either, but that was no reason for Dawna to be so rude.

"Actually," Dawna said, "I'm really feeling kind of sad today. I'm bummed about all that bad stuff that's been going on at the college. My sister goes there, and she said there was a big plot to murder that poor teacher. She told me that a lot of people were in on it. They were some students who hated Mr. Dudley so much that they had already made plans to dispose of his body."

Lisa glared at Dawna. "Whoever told you all that is crazy. Mr. Dudley isn't dead. He's just a bitter old cripple who's become senile. Maybe he just got tired of his rotten students and took off somewhere. Maybe he doesn't know *himself* where he is," she said.

"Well, they found his blood all over," Dawna persisted. "I don't think that's so easily explained by saying nasty things about the poor man."

There was fire in Lisa's eyes when she turned to Tony. "Your girlfriend really has a chip on her shoulder, doesn't she? What's her problem?"

"Yeah," Mac joined in suspiciously, "you been telling her stuff about us,

Tony? You saying we had something to do with Dudley disappearing?"

"I never said anything like that," Tony sputtered defensively. He knew he looked bad. Why would Dawna be so hostile and nasty if she didn't have reason to believe that Mac and Lisa had had something to do with Dudley's disappearance? And how did she know anything at all about them unless Tony had spilled the beans?

"I want to go home now," Dawna snapped, yanking up her towel with enough force to spray sand all over Mac and Lisa.

"Hey, you little witch!" Mac yelled. "Don't throw sand all over my girlfriend like that!"

Dawna ignored him. She started walking across the sand toward the steps leading up to the street. Mac grabbed Tony's shoulders. "Hey, man, you've been talking trash about us, haven't you? You told your little friend that we wasted Dudley, didn't you? Have you been talking to the cops, too? Admit it, man. You must have been running off at the mouth about that fight we had with the old codger."

"I haven't been talking to anybody," Tony snapped.

"'Well, I'm warning you that two can play that game, man. *I* can tell them about that original fiction story you wrote in Ms. Caufield's English lit class—the one about the vengeful student who killed his teacher in merry old England. You remember that story, don't you? Your hero got clean away with it because they never found a body," Mac said in a menacing voice.

"Hey, that was just a creative writing assignment, man," Tony snapped. "Ms. Caufield wanted a mystery written in the first person."

"Yeah, but *you* were the only one who wrote about killing a teacher over bad test scores, Tony," Mac said threateningly. "Who knows? Maybe it was a rehearsal for wiping out Dudley. You start talking trash to the cops about us, and *we* got some trash to give them, too. Believe it!" Mac snarled.

Tony pulled free of Mac. "You're nuts, man! Just get outta my face!" he shouted. Then he turned and walked toward the steps to the parking lot. When he came walking up, Dawna was waiting impatiently at the VW.

"So . . . did you enjoy your cozy little goodbye chat with those disgusting jerks?" Dawna snarled. "I'm sick and tired of standing here cooling my heels, waiting for you to finish up with your friends and unlock the darn car!"

Tony's usually calm nature quickly boiled over. "I'm sick and tired, too, Dawna—of your crummy attitude! You deliberately started a fight with people I see every day in school, and I don't appreciate it!"

Dawna began to cry. "What's wrong

with you? Do you want to be *pals* with people who probably murdered a teacher? And now you're furious with me for ruining your wonderful friendship with those creeps?"

"Dawna, you're acting like a jackass!" Tony exploded.

Shocked at his outburst, Dawna drew back her hand and slapped Tony across the face. Then she stood toe to toe with him, glaring in his face, and crying out hysterically, "You big coward! You'd just love to hit me back, wouldn't you? Your face is just so twisted with hate. Maybe *you* were mixed up in that plot to kill Mr. Dudley, too! I don't think I ever knew you at all, Tony Young! I'm just glad I found out what you're really like before it's too late!" Then her shoulders began to shake and she started sobbing uncontrollably.

Tony was numb with anger and humiliation. His face still smarted from the stinging blow. He yanked his wallet from his pocket, peeled off a $20 bill, and angrily threw it on the ground at Dawna's feet.

"Get a cab, lady! There's a payphone just ten feet away. Here's a little change to pay for the call. You're not going home with me!" He threw down some quarters along with the bill. Then he stormed over to the driver's side of the VW, got in, and drove off, leaving Dawna standing there with a look of absolute disbelief on her face.

"Great going," Tony sarcastically muttered to himself as he drove toward home. Now he'd broken up with his girlfriend over this missing teacher fiasco. Weren't things already bad enough? Mr. Dudley was ruining three days a week with his lousy class. Now, even when the old geezer was out of the picture, he was still ruining Tony's life!

Chapter 5

Tony thought about everything that had happened. He was now on the outs with Mac and Lisa. They were absolutely certain that he was talking trash about them. And when Lisa got to Brandi, she would feel the same way.

Tony stopped at Chaz's place on the way home. "What're you hearing about this Dudley thing, Chaz?" Tony asked. "It sure has messed up my life. Mac and Lisa think I'm ratting on them, and I had a big fight with Dawna over it."

"You broke up with Dawna?" Chaz asked, his eyes wide with amazement. "Oh, man, if I had a babe who looked that good, *nothing* would break us up!"

"Ahhh, she's got an attitude. She was determined to start something with Lisa and Mac, and she ended up slapping me in the face," Tony groaned. "I left her at the beach with cab fare. I was so mad I couldn't even drive her home."

"You didn't smack her back, did you, man?" Chaz asked.

"No way. I'm not that kind of guy," Tony said.

"Well, I heard the cops are coming to school tomorrow to have another talk with everybody who was in Dudley's class. It seems like bad things had been happening to Dudley even *before* he disappeared. Dudley told his son that somebody had messed with his car brakes, and almost got him killed. Then a few days later, somebody put an explosive device in his mailbox—so it looks like somebody *was* mad enough to do the old guy in," Chaz said.

"Listen, Chaz, you don't think Mac and Lisa and Brandi actually *did* something to Dudley, do you?" Tony asked. "I know those guys can be a pain sometimes, but you don't think—"

"I dunno, man," Chaz said. "I know that *I* hated old Dudley when I'd get back a bad grade on one of his unfair tests. Dudley kind of enjoyed flunking people, you know. He seemed to be almost proud of the kids he flunked. I overheard him one time talking to that English teacher, Caufield. He was chuckling and kind of bragging that 75 percent of the kids who flunked out of college had failed his world history class! He said they were spoiled losers who had no discipline or sense of duty. He didn't think they deserved to get a college degree.

"I know that Mac needs a passing grade in Dudley's class to stay in school. Brandi is close to flunking out, too. It's a bad scene, man! All these kids going after that college degree, and there's old Dudley standing in their way like a ten-foot concrete roadblock."

"But *murder*?" Tony gasped. "You

really think they'd resort to murder?"

"Hey, a lot of ordinary people commit murder," Chaz pointed out. "I read somewhere that only criminal types rob banks and do burglaries, but it's different with murder. Even normal people do murders. You know— something happens and they just *snap*."

When Tony went to school the next day, he wanted to avoid Mac, Lisa, and Brandi. But they were all in his English class, glaring at him during Ms. Mosko's lecture on Jane Austen's writing style. After class, Tony had to meet the police detective in the conference room.

As Tony walked out the door, Brandi came up and whispered fiercely, "Don't get us in trouble!"

Tony took a seat opposite the sallow-faced, bored-looking detective. He'd been talking to college kids all morning, and none of them had known very much. Now the detective glanced up at Tony, figuring that he wasn't likely to know anything either. "So, you're in Mr. Dudley's class, eh?" he asked.

"Yes," Tony said.

"Did you observe a lot of animosity toward Mr. Dudley in the classroom?" the detective asked.

"Yeah. Nobody liked him. He's real boring, and his tests were unfair because he never lectured on the material he quizzed us on. He'd talk about his personal life and then flunk people for not doing well on the tests," Tony said.

"Do you know anything about a plot to harm Mr. Dudley? Did you hear rumors or gossip—anything like that?" The detective's blue eyes now seemed to be drilling into Tony's face.

"No. Everybody just moaned about how much they hated him. But after he disappeared, there was gossip about plots and stuff—but I think that's all crazy," Tony said.

"Okay," the detective said, "you can go now, but we may get back to you."

He jotted something down on a pad.

Chaz Spender was in the conference room with the detective a lot longer than Tony was. He had actually seen the trio of suspected students in a heated argument with Dudley. He had watched them follow Dudley out to his car. And he had heard the students telling Dudley that he should be dead.

Chaz told the detective everything he knew. When he finally came out of the conference room, Tony was out in the hall, waiting for him.

"Well," Tony asked, "what went down in there?"

Chaz shrugged. "I might have put a noose around their necks," he said. "I didn't *want* to do it. But I had to tell the truth, right? I saw what I saw. Mac and those girls went after the old crud all the way to his car—and afterward, they seemed real scared."

Chapter 6

Tony and Chaz went for pizza at the place where Tony worked. Tony didn't have to go on duty for another half hour, so they had time to talk.

"The detective's face lit up when I told him," Chaz reported. "I figure Mac and the girls are gonna be invited down to the police station real soon. I don't take any delight in that. I've got nothing against those guys. I mean, in a way they did us all a favor if they . . . you know . . . got him outta here. But if they did it, they're gonna be busted.

"I hated Dudley, too. The man was the worst teacher who ever lived— and a heartless human being, too! But you can't just go crazy and murder somebody, even for a good reason."

Tony shook his head in puzzlement. "You notice how we always talk about the guy like he's gone for good?" he asked. "Why do we do that? We don't know for sure that he's dead."

"He *is*, Tony," Chaz insisted. "I feel it in my bones. When I saw the looks on those kids' faces the other day, I knew something heavy had gone down. I can sense death. Even when I was little, I could. If we were driving in the country and we'd come on an accident, I'd know if somebody had died there. It's like a sixth sense." Chaz sighed and took a big bite of pizza.

"But you didn't hear any shots, did you?" Tony asked. "They couldn't have shot him. Maybe they used a knife. Or maybe they bludgeoned him . . . but I just can't see it."

"He was an old man, Tony. An over-the-hill scrawny old man who was too lame to run away. Maybe they just gave him one big whack and it did him in.

He should've quit teaching *years* ago! It's too bad. I don't know why he stayed at it. He must've known he was no good at teaching anymore. And he must have had a good pension built up after so many years," Chaz said sadly.

"Must be terrible for his family not knowing where he is," Tony said, "or even if he's dead or alive. They can't even have a funeral until they know for sure. His wife must be going through a lot. I suppose he had grown kids."

"Yeah, he had a son, but no wife. She died years ago. I heard she was killed in a car accident. People who knew him way back when—like my dad—say that he changed a lot after that. Dad said that *he* had Dudley for history 25 years ago, and the guy was great. Sharp, interesting, really connecting with the students. That's not the guy *we* knew— the one who'd pass out tests with F's on them and smile like he was doing something great," Chaz said.

Tony shook his head. Then he put on his Pizzaman cap and headed off for the delivery truck. After he finished his shift, he went to his parents' house for dinner. Chaz had eaten a lot of pizza that afternoon, but Tony only had coffee. He was sick of pizza. He had been saving his stomach for Mom's homemade meatloaf with baked potatoes and string beans in butter sauce.

Over dinner, Tony and his parents talked about a lot of things, but the conversation eventually turned to the disappearance of Mr. Dudley.

"He's that really cranky teacher you told me about, isn't he, Anthony?" Mom asked as she loaded Tony's plate with second helpings.

"His wife was a lovely lady," Mom went on. "She'd always buy avocados and special onion bagels at our store. We felt so bad when she was killed. Mr. Dudley came in the store a few times after her death—but he was a changed

43

man. Then we never saw him again."

"How did the accident happen?" Tony asked.

"She was crossing a street on campus to bring her husband his lunch. The police said that a car struck her and killed her instantly. It was hit-and-run. The accident was witnessed by about a dozen students, but nobody got the license plate number. That last time Mr. Dudley came in the store, he talked about it. He said he thought some of the witnesses *knew* who was driving the car—that it was a fellow student—but they were unwilling to rat on their friend," Mom said.

After he got home that night, Tony thought about what Chaz had said. *It wasn't the war—Dudley's personality had changed when his wife died.* Mom had said the same thing. Maybe that was when Mr. Dudley got mean. Maybe that's what turned him from a fine, caring teacher into a nasty old curmudgeon who enjoyed flunking his students. Maybe that's why he had turned against *all* college students—because he thought one of them had killed his beloved wife. After that, Mr. Dudley probably figured that it was him against them. The students were his enemies.

It was easy to see how it could become a vicious circle. The more Dudley hated his students, the worse he was at teaching, and the more the kids hated him.

When Tony got home that night, the phone was ringing.

"Yeah?" he said, grabbing the phone.

"Tony, I'm so sorry about what happened," Dawna said. "I've been trying to get you all afternoon and evening. I'm just so sorry that I lost my temper. I never should have slapped you. Can you ever forgive me?"

"Yeah," Tony muttered, "sure, it's okay. Stuff happens." But, in truth, Tony would never forget what she had done.

Dawna already had a lot of traits Tony didn't like. She was okay for a casual date, although the girl he eventually would settle on had to be a lot different from Dawna. But the real deal-breaker was when she'd hauled off and smacked him. When that had happened, he knew for sure that he and Dawna wouldn't be together much longer. Tony couldn't stand violent people. It was okay to yell sometimes—but civilized people didn't *hit*.

"Tony, let me buy you breakfast tomorrow morning at the pancake house—the new place that serves those Belgian crepes you like so much," Dawna said. "We could meet there around nine, okay?"

"Okay," Tony said. Even though he had soured on Dawna, he didn't want to hurt her feelings. There was no need to cut her loose in a brutal way. He figured that he'd gradually see less and less of her, and just let the relationship die off.

Or maybe if he was lucky, she'd meet another guy and he'd be off the hook. Tony didn't like to hurt anybody's feelings if he didn't have to—even those of a girl who had acted like a jackass.

How could she have accused him? He would *never* have been one of the students screaming at old Dudley. Even though he felt the same as everybody else about him, it just wasn't Tony's style.

Early the next morning Tony got a call from Chaz. Just as they suspected, Mac and the two girls had been called to police headquarters. But now there was another new development. "Dudley's son found a sort of diary the old guy kept," Chaz said. "He turned it over to the police, and told the news media about it, too. Dudley Junior is real ticked off that a group of students would actually strike out at his father."

"So, Chaz, does anybody know what's in the diary?" Tony asked.

"I got a buddy who works at the TV

station. He said it's gonna be the big story on the six o'clock news. The stuff in his diary is supposed to be dynamite. Old Dudley accused the kids in his world history class of plotting violence against him," Chaz said.

"Oh, man, please tell me you're not serious!" Tony groaned. "That could make us *all* look bad!"

"Yeah. According to my buddy, Dudley said just about everybody in the class knew about the plot against him. He named specific names, too—guys he thought were the ringleaders," Chaz went on excitedly.

"*Names?*" Tony gasped. "Do you have any idea who he named?"

"No, the station isn't going to use names. I guess they could get in legal trouble if they went public with unproven accusations. But I wouldn't be surprised if *we're* on the list, Tony," Chaz said.

Tony remembered Dudley's classes—

how the old teacher would appear to be writing it down when somebody made a snide remark. Maybe he kept track of *everything*! His beady little eyes continually darted around the room all the time he was talking.

Then there were a couple students who were bootlickers, toadies. They guaranteed good grades for themselves by being syrupy sweet to Dudley. Tony thought it was very likely that they had tipped him off as to which students hated him.

"You know, Chaz, I never dissed Dudley to his face—but we all talked about him. And there were lots of times I'd be so bored I'd yawn all over the place or stare at the spiders making webs over in the corner," Tony said.

"Well, like I said, man," Chaz said nervously, "we're probably on the list. No doubt we'll get our chance to go down to police headquarters ourselves before very long."

Chapter 7

"Look, Chaz, I don't need to hear this," Tony groaned, "especially not at seven in the morning. I gotta meet Dawna for breakfast pretty soon, and that's bad enough—but now I've got old Dudley weighing on my mind, too."

Dawna waved frantically when she saw Tony, guiding him across the cavernous restaurant to a little corner table. Tony walked over and sat down, forcing a smile.

"Oh, Tony, I'm so glad you came! I've just been so upset over the way I acted. I wasn't feeling well, you know, and I think that's why I blew up. I hope you can forgive me because I really care for you a lot, and I'm so ashamed of myself," Dawna went on and on.

"That's okay, Dawna. Some of it was my fault, too," Tony said. "Let's just forget about it. I said some bad things, too. So let's just chalk it up to a bad day, okay?"

"Okay, but I had no right to slap you," Dawna said, nibbling at her Belgian crepe. She never ate much. She was terrified of putting more than a hundred pounds on her 5'1" frame. She was so thin that sometimes Tony thought she looked sick.

"Let it go, Dawna," Tony said. "I've already forgotten about it, all right?"

"Have you *really*?" Dawna asked, her face clouded by doubt.

"Sure," Tony said, smiling at her. But inside, Tony realized that he'd never liked the girl very much. That was sad because it was quite clear that she liked him a lot. For some reason, Tony felt a little guilty about his negative feelings. He had just wanted to have fun, surfing with a pretty girl and hanging out. He had never wanted it to get serious—but lately, Dawna was sticking to him like flypaper.

"Tony, you have such a strange look on your face," Dawna said anxiously. "Don't you love me anymore?"

Tony's spirits deflated like a burst balloon. If he could have chosen the *last* question he wanted to hear from Dawna, that would have been it. He had counted on her being smart enough never to ask such a thing. But she was dumber than he thought. The distaste in his eyes gave her the hint that something was wrong— but she had no idea just *how* wrong.

"Uh, no, it's not that, Dawna," Tony sputtered. "We're, uh . . . friends, right? Nothing has changed there."

Dawna stared hard at him, her eyes darkening with tears.

"Dawna, uh . . . *love* is a pretty serious word. I don't think we've even known each other long enough to talk about . . . you know, *love*, right?" Tony laughed a hollow laugh. "You know . . .

love . . . hey, that's a big thing, right? But you and me, we're good friends. . . ."

"But Tony, I really love you," Dawna insisted, fighting back tears.

"No, no, you don't. You're just a kid! Why, you don't know what you want. I'm only 22 myself, and I'm really immature," Tony babbled. "Man, I don't know *anything*! Sometimes I'm a real goof-up. The two of us, Dawna, we're just a couple of kids playing in the sand on the beach, that's all . . . and hey, that's good! That's really . . . very . . . good," he stammered.

A stricken, almost tragic look came over Dawna's face. "I knew it. You don't love me anymore. You *used* to love me. You know you did. It's because of what happened at the beach. You can't forgive me," Dawna wept.

"Come on, Dawna, that's not it. I told you I had forgotten all about that. I've got other things on my mind. Everybody in school is worried about that Dudley thing. I am too," Tony said, desperately trying to change the subject.

"Oh, Tony . . . were you mixed up in that big plot to kill the teacher? I was afraid of that! You're so burdened with guilt that you don't have room in your heart for love! Tony, listen, I'll help you. I don't care what you've done. We'll get through this together," Dawna cried.

"No, I didn't do anything to Dudley, I swear it!" Tony cried. He had the horrible sense of being trapped. Dawna's intensity was like a huge, wet, warm blanket weighing him down, smothering him. Almost before his eyes, the petite young woman sitting in front of him had turned into a monster, longing to swallow him up.

"Dawna, come on, please! Get a grip. I don't even *know* anything about what happened to Dudley. That business has nothing to do with you and me. Long before Dudley disappeared, I was afraid that we were spending too much time together. Listen to me: I don't want to be in love with *anybody*, Dawna—not yet. I'm too young."

Slowly and dramatically, tears began to spill from Dawna's eyes and roll down her cheeks. "I . . . I could tell when we were s-surfing . . . I could tell you'd ch-changed . . . You got too upset when you talked about that teacher. The t-truth is you're feeling guilty! It's like that Russian story, *Crime and Punishment*—how the g-guy kept agonizing over this murder," Dawna whimpered miserably.

Tony had eaten about half his Belgian crepe, but he couldn't eat another bite. Now he just wanted to get out of this restaurant and breathe some fresh air. He wanted to get away from Dawna Reston as fast as he could.

"Well, I gotta get going," Tony said, jumping up so quickly he almost knocked over his chair.

Dawna began to sob loudly.

Tony knew he should stay and try to

console her, but he just *couldn't*. They had come in separate cars, so he just ran out to his VW and never looked back.

"How did I get into this?" Tony asked himself as he was driving off. He had met Dawna at a concert featuring the old hits of the dead country rocker, Gram Parsons. Dawna was pretty. That's all that mattered to Tony then. Then it turned out that they both liked jazz and the same kind of movies. After their first few dates, she had said she was dying to learn to surf. Since Tony was an expert surfer, it just seemed natural that they should become friends.

It had all started out so nice and simple. Tony had wanted a pretty girlfriend, nothing deep or permanent. Now he just wanted to forget about Dawna, so he flipped on his radio to a heavy metal station. Maybe some brain-blasting music would drive away the image of Dawna's weeping.

A news bulletin came on right away.

"There may be a break in the puzzling disappearance of college professor Walter Dudley. Although police are refusing to confirm or deny the report, reliable sources say that bloodstained clothing belonging to the history teacher was located in a dumpster not far from the college parking lot where he was last seen," the newsman said in a dramatic voice.

"*Oh, no!*" Tony groaned aloud.

That evening the television news programs told more about the blood-stained clothing as well as the diary that Mr. Dudley had left behind. In the diary entries quoted, Mr. Dudley claimed that he was being persecuted because he demanded good work from his students and refused to accept their shoddy work. The diary went on to describe secret meetings at which a number of students had plotted against him.

Later on, Chaz called Tony at his apartment.

"Hey, man, listen fast, 'cause I'm not staying on the line long. *Mac and Brandi confessed!* Lisa just told me. They're trying to cut a deal with the district attorney by implicating the rest of us. I'm scared. Mac and Brandi are going to be telling such a pack of lies that we'll all end up in the slammer for conspiracy to murder. I'm not sticking around and waiting for the cops to rap on my door. I'm outta here, man—and if you got any sense, you'll do the same," Chaz said.

Tony broke out in a cold sweat. He remembered that ridiculous story he had written last year, the one describing a student killing his teacher. Now that story could be used against him. Mac and Brandi would tell the cops *anything* to sweeten their deal with the DA!

Tony's mind whirled. How could this be happening? Mac and Brandi weren't murderers! Maybe the cops pressured them too much, and they'd just snapped! It probably seemed that the only way to stop the questioning was to tell a pack of lies. Tony had read stories where that had happened to people.

Tony felt trapped in a terrible nightmare that went on and on . . . that just kept getting worse. . . .

Chapter 8

Tony couldn't see the sense of running away like Chaz was doing. If the cops came after him, that would just make him look even more guilty!

For several minutes, he sat in his chair, his face in his hands. Mac and Brandi couldn't have murdered Dudley. But *something* had happened . . . and if the old guy hadn't been murdered, where was he?

Then Tony got a hunch, seemingly out of nowhere.

About six months ago, Mr. Dudley had taken his world history students on a field trip. In spite of his limp, the old man had led everybody down into a rugged canyon. He claimed there were Indian artifacts in the area. The students did find some old clay shards, but many kids were snickering behind their hands about the pottery being made in China.

The field trip ended in an old cabin near an archeological dig. Earlier, Mr. Dudley had said that he owned a cabin in the area and would serve everyone refreshments there after the long, hot trip down the canyon and back up again. But all they got were crackers and warm water. Looking back on that fiasco now, Tony figured it was just another way Dudley had found to spite his students. Tony's classmates had laughed about it for months after. *Dudley's dud field trip* is what they called it.

It was the memory of that day that gave Tony his hunch. That's why he was now in his VW heading for that cabin. Tony had forgotten that the last mile was a rutted dirt road. Mr. Dudley had used a large van to transport the 12 students who had gone on the field trip. Now the road was even more rutted than it had been then, but Tony kept on going.

Finally, he reached the cabin and stopped to look around. He figured there was at least a *chance* that Dudley was hiding up here, trying to make as much trouble as he could for the students he despised. He went to the front door and pounded on the ancient wood frame.

"Mr. Dudley! Are you in there?" Tony shouted. "You trying to make everybody believe you're dead so we'll all get in trouble?" Tony was shaking. He didn't know whether his hunch was right or not, but he had a strong feeling that somebody was hiding inside the cabin. At least someone *had* been there. The outside faucet was dripping as if it had recently been used, and fresh bird seed was in a feeder.

If Mac and Brandi had killed Mr. Dudley in the campus parking lot, what had happened to the body? The kids had been on foot. There wasn't any way for them to carry Dudley away without being seen.

"Come on out now. The game is up, Mr. Dudley. . . ."

"Don't you move," Dudley's voice crackled behind Tony. When he turned to look, Tony found himself staring directly into the old man's rifle. Dudley's face was twisted in an angry scowl. "You're trespassing on my property, Tony Young. I've got every right in the world to shoot you right now—do you know that?"

Mr. Dudley's voice sizzled with rage.

Chapter 9

"Hey, Mr. Dudley, I just had to find out if you were dead or alive," Tony gasped. "A couple of students are already being held by the police for murdering you—and here you are, alive and well!"

"You march into the cabin, Young, while I decide what to do with you," Dudley snapped.

Tony went inside the cabin and sat at the kitchen table. Dudley sat opposite him, still holding the rifle. "I must say I'm pleased to hear that those punks are under arrest," Mr. Dudley said.

"But . . . you're okay," Tony said.

"I am *far* from okay, you useless wretch! You—and people like you—have ruined my life. One of your fellow students snatched the light from my world when my dear wife was run down and killed in her prime. And ever since then, you've turned my teaching career into a hateful ordeal," Dudley growled, his hands still gripping the rifle that was leveled at Tony's chest.

"Look, I'm really sorry—" Tony started to say.

"Are you? That's a lie. I often saw you in class, stretching and yawning. Oh, yes, you waved your arms in the air when you stretched so all your friends could see how bored you were. Do you think I'm *blind*?" Dudley demanded.

"Look, Mr. Dudley, I'm sorry about all that—but, you know, it's against the law to fake your own murder and get innocent people in trouble. You're a smart man, Mr. Dudley. You gotta know that it's downright illegal to pull a stunt like that," Tony said.

Dudley laughed bitterly. "Ah, but I've done nothing wrong. On that fateful

Monday, your friends followed me from my classroom and proceeded to insult me shamefully. I was hurrying to my car when that thug, Mac, grabbed my coat and caused my leg to give way. I stumbled and fell into my car, striking my head on the rearview mirror. I was dazed. Blood was streaming from the wound. I heard those vile girls, Brandi and Lisa, prattling in frightened little twitters, 'Oh, you've killed the old fool, Mac. Oh, Mac, let's get outta here. He's bleeding to death!'"

"Then it *was* an accident," Tony gasped in relief.

"No! They laid their filthy hands on my coat! They had no right to do that. I thought to myself, 'Well, they hate me enough to have killed me, so why shouldn't I let them think they did?' When they left, I hurried off, put my bloody shirt and coat in the dumpster, and wrote out some accusations . . . I was *entitled* to my revenge. As a matter of fact, I enjoyed the whole thing immensely," Dudley said with a smirk.

"But they've confessed now, Mr. Dudley. I mean, they were under so much pressure they confessed to something they didn't do—murdering you! This is wrong!" Tony cried. "And pointing that rifle at me is wrong, too, so why don't you put it down?"

"I haven't decided yet if I should shoot you as a trespasser. As for those punks, let them sweat. They certainly made *me* sweat every time I walked into the classroom. With their taunting looks, their snickers, their rude remarks—oh, how they tormented me! And their kind killed my Barbara, my beautiful Barbara who was the kindest, sweetest soul who ever lived," Dudley cried out.

"Mr. Dudley, not all kids are jerks. You've got a son, right? I bet *he's* not a jerk," Tony said, taking another tack to make the old man relent.

The old man's mood changed

abruptly. "Bob is a wonderful young man," he said softly.

"Is he in on this faked murder, Mr. Dudley?" Tony asked.

"Of course not!" Dudley snapped. "I wouldn't involve my son in a scheme to exact my own vengeance. My life is almost over, but Bob's has just begun," he went on, a tenderness coming into his voice for the first time.

"So your son thinks you're dead, too, huh?" Tony asked softly. "That's a pretty dirty trick to play on someone who loves you, man."

For just a second Walter Dudley looked conscience-stricken. He turned toward the cellular phone on the end table. Tony could see the man's brain working behind the distressed confusion in his eyes. In his furious desire to punish his students, Dudley had never thought about the anguish he was causing his son.

"Don't move while I'm calling," Dudley warned, snatching up the phone.

Chapter 10

"Bobby?" Mr. Dudley said in a shaky voice. "Yes, I'm all right. I'm sorry, Bobby. I should have called you sooner, but I didn't want to involve you." A tear ran down the old professor's face. "I know that, Bobby. And I love you, too... In the cabin, yes... I'm fine... I've got everything I need right here. Listen, Bobby, don't tell anyone that I'm alive. I want those punks to sweat for a while longer. They deserve it. I must go now. Goodbye, Bobby."

Dudley put down the phone and heaved a sigh.

"I never realized what I was doing to him! Perhaps I *am* losing it. There's just been too much grief, too much abuse at the hands of the heartless young. It may be true ... perhaps I am bent beyond repair. . . ." the man's voice trailed off.

"Mr. Dudley, you've got to let me go. Holding someone against his will is called kidnapping. It's a serious crime," Tony said.

"Trespassing is a crime, too," Mr. Dudley snorted. "I'll just say that I had to hold you until the police could arrest you as a prowler," Dudley said.

"Good, then call the police," Tony said. He was desperately hoping that Bobby Dudley was on his way. Surely he would be concerned enough about his father's welfare to come to the cabin immediately. That phone call must have shown him how distraught and irrational the old man had become.

Mr. Dudley kept the rifle trained on Tony as he rambled on about all the miserable days and years he had spent teaching rude, ungrateful students.

Then, suddenly, a sports utility vehicle pulled up outside. "Dad!" Bob

Dudley shouted, bursting into the cabin. He stared, frightened, at the rifle in his father's hands. Then, looking confused, he glanced over at Tony.

"Bobby, you shouldn't have come here," Mr. Dudley cried, the rifle wavering in his grasp.

The younger man gently took the rifle from his father. Then he looked at Tony. "Hey, I'm sorry about all this. Are you okay? You want me to call the cops?" he asked.

"No. I'll just split. You handle it from here," Tony said, hurrying outside to his VW. He was in a cold sweat as he drove down the mountain.

Mr. Dudley was taken to a hospital for a complete checkup. The blow he had suffered to his head when he fell into the rearview mirror had stunned him. Perhaps that head trauma had contributed to his bizarre behavior, the doctors said. No charges were filed. Mr. Dudley retired immediately and went to a resort for a long recuperation.

Mac and Brandi had never confessed to murdering the old man. They had only admitted causing Mr. Dudley to fall. They said they had left the scene out of fear that he was seriously hurt. But no charges were filed against them, either. Clearly, Mr. Dudley's fall had been an accident. The three students had only meant to stop Mr. Dudley so they could talk.

When Tony took Dawna surfing on Sunday, a really handsome surfer boy named Jake Dumont caught her eye. As she flirted and giggled at Jake's attention, Tony fled, hitting a six-foot wave. In a moment he was flying in the water and feeling free as the wind.

Really free at last.

COMPREHENSION QUESTIONS

RECALL

1. What class did Mr. Dudley teach?

2. What surprised Tony about Mac and Lisa's behavior when they were surfing?

3. According to Tony's mother, how did Mr. Dudley react to his wife's death?

4. Why did Tony tell Dawna he didn't want to get married?

VOCABULARY

1. Lisa told Dawna that Mr. Dudley was *senile*. What does *senile* mean?

2. Tony hated Mr. Dudley's class because the old man was boring and *dictatorial*. What does *dictatorial* mean?

3. Tony said that Mr. Dudley lectured in a *monotone*. What is a *monotone*?

WHO AND WHERE?

1. Where did Tony work?

2. Who first warned Tony to say nothing to the police?

3. Where did Tony eventually find Dudley?

4. Who suspected Tony's involvement in a murder plot?

5. Who took Mr. Dudley's rifle away from him?

CAUSE AND EFFECT

1. What was the *cause* of so many failures on Mr. Dudley's tests?

2. Dawna slapped Tony's face. What *effect* did that have on him?

3. Mr. Dudley had decided that all students were his enemies. What was the *cause* of this decision?

ANALYZING CHARACTERS

1. Which two words could be used to describe Tony Young? Explain your reasoning.
   - *perplexed*
   - *hot-tempered*
   - *sensible*

2. Which two words could be used to describe Walter Dudley? Explain why you think so.
   - *stable*
   - *vindictive*
   - *grieving*

3. Which two words could be used to describe Dawna Reston? Explain your reasoning.
   - *childish*
   - *brilliant*
   - *insecure*

DRAWING CONCLUSIONS

1. What conclusion did Chaz draw about Mr. Dudley's disappearance?

2. What conclusion did Tony draw about Mr. Dudley's phone call to his son?